Little Lady Full Copy

G. M. Lamond

1.

"Don't you dare sneak out like you did last time, Cliff Bright!" Lucy Agnes looked straight at Cliff.

"What do you mean?" Cliff acted innocent, and hurt. He knew when she added the "Bright," she was serious.

"You weren't there for the last vaccines, and so she only associates me with the pain."

Cliff knew this was true. He had left the room because he could not stand the sight of needles, let alone one puncturing skin, his or anyone else's. "You know I faint dead away when I even see a needle. Once did it watching a movie."

Lucy was unforgiving. "This time you stay! Man up or I'll man you up!"

Felicity Agatha, now almost three, who had been listening, ran across the reception area to her mom and dad. It was time for her two-year catch-up vaccines.

Cliff looked at her and wondered aloud. "When and where do you get all this energy, rolling, running, talking, laughing, jumping, bouncing!"

Felicity acted as if she did not hear him. She pointed a little finger at them both. Shaking it like a schoolmarm, she scolded them, "Don't you fussing," she said, and then repeated, "Don't you fussing!"

She's the boss of us," Cliff said, "and I wonder who put her in charge?"

Lucy was not to be distracted and she was not apologetic. She looked at Cliff with her You-better-do-what-I-say-and-do-it-now face. Then she addressed Felicity. "Sometimes, darling, your daddy needs some encouragement."

Felicity tried to repeat the long word. "In curgage?"

Lucy smiled. Like a mom, she thought, *Incredible language development for a two year old.* "Encouragement. Encouragement."

Felicity smiled back. "No, no mommy. Fussing! Don't you fussing!"

So smart, Cliff thought, *so intuitive. So full of love.* They were all so wrong when they counseled them to "terminate it."

He thought back to that time when so much pressure had been brought to bear on him and Lucy to "terminate the pregnancy" for their happiness, for their future children not yet here. No other happiness, no other persons mattered. *But*, he had thought, *we never could ever again have this child, this unique little human being, her smile, her hugs, and her love.*

2.

Before Felicity's birth, several doctors and nurses had "counseled" them.

"In scientific language," Doctor Lena Wendt, the obstetrician assigned to them, had said, "There is a complete extra copy of chromosome 21. This is Down Syndrome."

Not "this child has" or "your baby has," but simply "there is" as if that was all there was to the reality happy within Lucy, no baby elephant in the room, no human beings other than the doctor and the two of them. Cliff looked at Lucy and did not say a word.

"Normal human beings have 23 chromosome pairs, 46 total," the doctor continued. If you carry this to term, it will have 46 plus 1, an extra copy of number 21. And in this case it is what we call 'full copy'."

It, thought Lucy. "Full copy?"

"In some cases there is a partial copy, some a complete copy. This is a complete copy, an entire extra chromosome. "

Lucy was attentive and concerned, but not upset. She looked at Cliff and could see he too was not upset. "Do they know how this happens?"

"Yes, usually during sperm or egg development, the 21st chromosome does not separate as it should. When this affects all the cells in the body, they call it 'Down Syndrome'. When only some of the cells are affected, they call it 'mosaic' Down Syndrome. "

Lucy thought of their ride to the doctor's office and talking with Cliff about baby names, naming this "it," and how already "it" wasn't an "it," but their child, mommy's baby, daddy's baby, their baby.

"You said sperm or egg development," said Cliff. He did not want Lucy blaming herself for anything or even thinking the thought that maybe she had done something wrong. "This means it could be from either parent?"

"You heard me right," said the doctor. "And it can also happen after the sperm and egg have merged, so it's not initially present in either the sperm or the egg."

"I guess there is no reason to get a second opinion, is there?" Lucy asked.

"The false positive rate is somewhere between two to five percent, so you could run the test again. But you have to keep in mind the danger of you miscarrying with every test, and risk of infection for you. The dangers and risks diminish the longer you wait during pregnancy to do the test. You could test again in the third trimester and then decide."

Lucy thought, *I guess there is no danger of infection for 'it,' and I know what 'decide' means.*

Cliff looked at Lucy as he said, "No, there is no reason to re-test."

Lucy smiled.

Dr. Wendt completely misinterpreted Cliff's words, Lucy's smile, and her silence.

Five months later, Felicity was born. No one at the hospital could remember anyone having a live Down Syndrome baby there. They put Lucy with Felicity in their own room, with no one else.

"Full copy," Cliff said when he first held Felicity in the delivery room and looked into her eyes. "You are Felicity Agatha, Full Copy of the image and likeness of God's love. I love you little girl."

He placed Felicity back on Lucy's stomach and she looked straight at Lucy whenever Lucy spoke. When Lucy said, "I love you, Felicity Agatha," Felicity would not take her eyes from her mother, nor from the voice she had heard all those months, warm in her mother's womb and safe in her mother's love.

3.

"There seems to be nothing about changing this. People just live with this. Kids just live with it and do the best they can," Lucy told Cliff as she looked up from her laptop screen. "It's like 'that's the way it is' and they all want to spend their time and their precious research dollars searching for cures and treatments for so many other things."

"But I found something, I guess by accident, natural medicine, nutrition, and something called 'essential oils.' No 'cure.' But more than hope for dealing with the physical and mental aspects of it all."

"What? Where? Sounds mumbo jumbo." Lucy was unbelieving.

"No, apparently not mumbo jumbo, not just drugs, but real medicine. And all kinds of treatments, and supplements, nutrition, immune system support, metabolic therapy, developmental therapy, cognitive and social training, and physical therapy."

"You've read all this?"

"No," Cliff replied, "But I've read some and I saw the tons of internet search results. Read a few. Enough to tell me we need to check it all out."

"You're going to find yourself married to an expert," said Lucy.

Lucy was unaware then that many stories about parents with a Down Syndrome child were the stories of mothers who had decided to do all they could to comfort and nourish and care for their own child. Their stories included resulting changes in the typical physical manifestations of Down Syndrome.

These characteristics can include decreased muscle tone, a flat nose, eyes slanting up or 'almond shaped' eyes, small ears and several other features. In addition to these physical characteristics, there are a variety of health issues that are more pronounced or more prevalent; e.g., pulmonary hypertension, seizures, heart holes, sleep apnea, autism, failure to thrive, poor immunity, and anemia.

"Hey," said Lucy, looking at her computer, "Here's a 'Trisomy Scientific Study Research Consortium' with members around the world. This one doctor says clearly this has never been called a 'disease,' and 'Down Syndrome' too is a misnomer. Since the cause is known, it's a 'condition,' not a 'syndrome' anymore. They've got a proactive and in some ways preventative approach. This isn't just drugs, this isn't 'palliative'."

"The way I see it, said Cliff, "there is a whole lot we can do for Felicity, and we have a lot to learn."

"More still here," said Lucy, looking away from the computer screen. "There's other kinds, other 'trisomies.'" She had been reading from another article on natural treatments. "There's trisomy 13 and 18, too. They have three copies of chromosomes 13 or 18, instead of the usual two copies. In all I've seen so far, there is more than a glimmer of hope. "

"That's all I need," said Cliff. "And Felicity here with us."

4.

As the intake clerk said "Felicity Bright, Cliff turned to Lucy.

"OK," said Cliff, "I'll go in with you, but I will sit down, just in case."

Felicity came over and hugged Cliff's leg. "Good daddy," she said, looking up at him and smiling.

Felicity had already had over twenty doses of nine different vaccines since she was born. Today, there were going to be multiple injections, another three compound doses in total.

5.

"Cliff, Cliff!" Lucy was screaming.

Cliff ran into Felicity's room. His first thought was that she was dead.

"She's not responding, hardly moving," cried Lucy.

Felicity lay in bed, on her back, staring at the ceiling, without acknowledging Lucy or Cliff. No smile. No laugh.

Cliff took her in his arms and still she did not look at him.

"Darling, darling, daddy's here." Relieved, he saw she was alive.

At the emergency room, nothing changed. Felicity remained nonresponsive and the staff had no explanation for what was going on. All her vital signs were normal.

One nurse and then a doctor checked her entire body for injury and broken bones. The law required this check for any child brought to the emergency room.

"Any falls, bumps, injuries, sickness, anything in the last few days?" the emergency room doctor asked.

"Nothing," said Lucy, "she had her three-year catch-up vaccines two days ago."

The doctor asked again, "No injuries, no falls, no cold, no cough, flu, no scrapes, nothing?"

Cliff was more than curious. "Why have you asked that same question again?"

"If there is no other explanation, and with the recent vaccine doses, the CDC requires us to make a vaccine 'adverse event' report. Probably no connection with the vaccines, but still federal law requires it."

"What do you mean, 'no connection'?" asked Lucy. There was worry in her voice.

"There is a growing mass of evidence, more and more, hard evidence, anyone who follows this knows it can no longer be ignored. There may be some connection with many conditions and even some diseases. The toxic metals, preservatives, and other things in vaccines. What's supposed to be there and what's not."

"Toxic?" Cliff asked, astounded.

"Different vaccines have different preservatives, carriers, and some different 'adjuvants.' Basically, they include some metals, some bad heavy metals that would be toxic in large enough amounts. Some vaccines have them so that any living contaminant that may be present cannot survive. Without them a great number of vaccines would not even be possible.

It's like using preservatives for food in the grocery store so they don't go rancid and so they have an acceptable, longer shipment, storage, and shelf life. Like sugar. That's why sugar, a preservative, is now in so many foods."

"Contaminants? Alive? Allowed amounts? Why are they there at all?" asked Cliff.

"It is not the case that materials in vaccines are outlawed, prohibited totally. Some are allowed, but in specified amounts. And, yes, live bacteria and viruses can be in vaccines. Even with the adjuvants and preservatives and toxic materials, vaccines have been recalled because they had deadly bacteria in them that was not killed. Once the polio vaccine was contaminated with a virus, simian virus, and there may be a cancer link with this virus. "

Cliff was unbelieving. "Metals? Toxic?"

"Yes, like aluminum, lead, mercury. Even stainless steel."

"In which vaccines?" Lucy wondered.

"Most of them. Has to be for mass production, preservation, and for provision in the millions of doses to large populations. One study of 44 samples of 29 different human vaccines, including those for influenza, meningitis, allergies, cervical cancer and hepatitis, found contaminants in all of them."

"Diseases?" asked Lucy.

"That's a long list," said the doctor. "Autism, ADHD, Gulf War Syndrome, AIDS, autoimmune diseases, cancer, MS, SIDS, neurodevelopmental diseases, diabetes and others. Some people go so far as to say that SIDS, sudden infant death syndrome, should be called VDS, vaccine death syndrome."

Lucy and Cliff looked at each other. "This is senseless," said Cliff.

"There is another terrible aspect of all this," said the doctor. "Why do you come here? To an emergency room? Why do you take your child to a doctor when he or she is sick? And you don't know what to do? Often it is because you don't know what this child has, what has caused this, what is 'this'? This is about your individual child and this child's symptoms and pains, right now, not any other child. But we herd children like cattle in a feed lot and, without checking each one out in detail, we give them all the same vaccines at the same time. Adults too."

Lucy stared at Cliff without speaking

The doctor continued. "Oh sure, there are a few preliminary questions, but you can walk right in to any drug store nationwide, right now, and get any number of vaccines, few or no questions asked. And, for example with the MMR vaccine, for little children, these vaccines can contain recombinant human albumin, fetal bovine serum, and chick embryo fibroblasts, with the potential for interspecies activation of unknown retroviruses, molecular mimicry, and reactivation of the virulence of the infectious virus itself. Hardly anyone studies and publicly reports on these medical risks."

"So why don't they run some tests or do some background checks or something for each person, each child, before they get a vaccine?" Lucy was incredulous.

"I know," said the doctor. "Seems to just be common sense, medical sense, doesn't it? There is typically no individualized risk assessment, no screening for personalized care based on lifestyle or genetic makeup, and often no checking for altered or deficient immunity when one gets a vaccine or had a child vaccinated. And there is more about each individual that is ignored. Deficient maternal diets of this or that particular child. The mother's regular intake of both prescription and nonprescription drugs, even ibuprofen and others. Formula consumed instead of breast milk. Maternal exposures to pesticides and herbicides, and scans and X-rays. We ignore any synergistic effects of any and all of this. It is as if we assume all the children are the same age, they all are in exactly the same physical condition, all the same size, and they are all going to the communal skatepark, and so all of them must have the same size pads, same size shoes, same skates, same size protective gear, and identical helmets which are forced onto each little head. This is not medicine. This is 'just business'. "

"And all the negative information, this is all public?" asked Lucy.

"Yes, somewhat, more and more. There was a study just a few years ago in a noted journal and the reported findings were that the researchers had found single particles like lead particles and agglomerations or assemblies like gold-zinc combinations of several unexplainable and toxic substances in vaccines. The researchers could not figure out where they were from. Some of them were micro-sized, some nano-sized. Some of them were not listed in the required list of the vaccine ingredients. Still, with all the money involved, and this is billions and billions of dollars, you can imagine what Big Vaxx does to stifle and censor the spread of information. And put out their own narrative worldwide. Often the morality of 'assume-the-risk-for–the-rest of us' and the 'common good' stories. It's like vaccine shaming."

Lucy was silent.

Cliff spoke. "You said 'Big Vaxx'?"

"You have heard about Big Tobacco, Big Sugar, Big Soda, Big Fluoride, and Big Pharma-all disparaging nicknames for the businesses, the amoral and immoral entities, some of them somewhat amorphous, that for years tried to cover up and then deny the injurious health effects of tobacco, sugar, sugared carbonated soft drinks, fluoridated water, and many prescription drugs. Bottom line, it was, it is for the bottom line, for money, pure and simple. Well, some folks now are labeling the entities who have a vested interest in the marketing and sale of vaccines as 'Big Vaxx.' Because of the pharmaceutical industry connections, some call it Big Pharma Vaxx. Others call it 'BB Vaxx,' Big Bad Vaxx'."

Cliff and Lucy were silent until Cliff asked a question.

"Doctor, do you have children?"

"Yes, two, ages three and five."

"Have you had them vaccinated regulary since birth?"

The doctor looked around the emergency room. No one else was within earshot.

"No," he said quietly," we have decided to wait. There is too much evidence, unexplained evidence, and we just decided to wait for more studies. And couple this with the incredible speed of the uptake rate of nutrients for young children — 'growth spurt' doesn't even begin to convey how they grow daily. I know many doctors and nurses, and others in the health care business who do not have their children vaccinated. Most are silent about it. Some have gone public."

"But don't they make you? The government? Schools? Somebody force you to do it?" asked Lucy incredulously.

"No, here, but not everywhere, you can opt out and get a government exemption. Got to get it notarized and do it every year or so. But you can do it. Luckily you can still do it here, but not in every state."

"Have you ever before seen any child hurt or injured by a vaccine?" Cliff had become very serious.

The doctor looked around the room again and then spoke. "We have, and everyone I know at every other hospital and emergency facility has too. It is so common that the federal government has set up the VICP, the federal Vaccine Injury Compensation Program, that provides damage awards to parents whose child is injured or who lose children to vaccine injury. So the vaccine manufacturers have no liability. The government has paid out over four billion dollars. In one recent case in which the government awarded damages, an autistic child had seven vaccines at one doctor visit, they wanted to save money and not make multiple visits, after which she developed autism."

Cliff walked over and took Felicity's hand in his. There was still no response and she continued to stare ahead.

The doctor continued. "The VCIP has paid for claims of vaccine injury for over twenty years now. The pharmaceutical companies do not pay for these claims. It's tax dollars. My money. Your money. Our money."

"I have never heard of any of this," said Cliff. "How do you know all this?"

"It's public. And my wife and I have a very real interest in this. Go to several government sites on line, You can find it quick, or dig just a little and read all this. You'll learn that over 1200 claims have been filed with the VCIP by family members for the death of a loved one claimed to be caused by vaccines. And you can find information about the claimed injuries related to vaccines. They include encephalopathy, anaphylactic shock, brachial neuritis, chronic arthritis, thrombocytopenic purpura, and paralytic polio intussusception, and any acute complication or what they call 'sequela'. And these include death."

"And right now you have found nothing wrong with Felicity?" Cliff asked.

"Nothing. Except the lack of attention, lack of focus, and some failure to respond to stimuli, lights, voices. We cannot explain this." The doctor was almost apologetic. "We can discharge her and you can take her home. There are several support groups for parents of these children. And I know you will get a lot of information about vaccines from some of them. Whether or not it is all true, you can judge. She is your child. I suggest you check it all out and learn all you can. There are many, many tests that can be run, scans that can be done, and They may or may not tell you something about the cause of this.”

“What sources have this information?” Cliff asked.

“You go on the internet and you will find more than you ever dreamed. And those office holders and politicians not supported by Big Pharma and Big Vaxx are starting to sit up and take notice.”

On the way home, with Felicity silent, still, staring out the car window at the lights flashing by, Lucy did not speak.

“What now?” Cliff asked.

“I don’t know,” was all that Lucy said.

“I know,” said Cliff. “We love this child. This child is God’s gift to us. A ‘full copy’ of His image and likeness, of His love. With Him, we loved her into being, and being here with us, and with Him we will love her, always. And that ‘always’ has just started, because we can love her now from here to all eternity.”

6.

Lucy and Cliff began spending hours and hours doing research at the library, and on the internet, and reading books and reports they had saved on their computers and some they had ordered in hard copy.

They learned that in some cases brain function was altered or diminished due to metals and other substances that were present in a mother before she gave birth. Some of this "congenital" toxic material was not from vaccines. Some was. But if it was there, and then coupled with what was in a vaccine for a child, the combination of the two amounts could render it present at a level sufficient to cause brain distortion, disease, neural injury, or brain damage. This was especially true in newborns and young children whose brains and bodies were still growing, and growing at lightning speed compared to growth later on in life.

Over the next few months, Felicity was not responsive, but she seemed to listen and to learn. Lucy and Cliff tried to speak to her as much as they had before. She would still sit still if they read a book in her presence, but without any apparent response to words and pictures, and without the joyful chatter and comments like she had done before.

They had test after test done, every scan, and every blood analysis. Forensic-type hair tests and tissue studies. Everything indicated that there were abnormal levels of some toxic metals present, including some in her brain, aluminum, and some others; but no one had any treatment or program to remove them or nullify their effects. They were told that nothing was possible due to the inherent issues with normal brain surgery and the size, tiny, often molecular-sized, deposits of the materials in her brain and in other body tissue.

"Have you noticed how she seems entranced when me and John play chess?" Cliff asked Lucy one day.

"John" was uncle John, Lucy's brother. Cliff and John were about equally matched in chess, so much so that long ago they quit keeping tabs on wins and losses.

"Yes," said Lucy. "Her focus and intensity are amazing."

7.

One day a few weeks before Felicity's fourth birthday, John and Cliff were into another game of chess and Felicity, quiet and intense, was in a chair watching it all.

Cliff made a move and said, "Take that! Think about that while I go to the bathroom!" He turned to Felicity. "Watch him!"

Cliff got up and walked out of the room as John studied the board. Felicity got out her chair and up into Cliff's.

John made a move and then noticed that Felicity continued to stare at the board.

"Darling, think you can do better than Daddy?" John laughed.

Felicity reached out to a pawn and moved it one space forward.

Cliff sat back in awe. It was a correct move for a pawn. Then he looked at the board. *Interesting move*, he thought. And then he studied the board some more.

When Cliff returned, he saw John's white king toppled on the board and John staring at Felicity.

As Felicity began, without looking up from the board, to replace all the pieces in their game-starting positions, John said, "Cliff, she mated me in six moves, six moves!"

"What? You tooling me around?" Cliff stared at John. Then he realized Felicity was putting the pieces in their correct positions. Once they were all in place, Felicity stayed in Cliff's chair, waiting.

"You give her a go!" said John.

Cliff moved into John's chair. *Is he pranking me?* Cliff thought. He chose a center pawn and moved it two spaces forward.

Felicity moved quickly, a pawn in reply to Cliff's pawn and then, just as quickly after Cliff moved another pawn, she moved a knight out in front of her pawns.

Twenty-one moves later, Cliff yelled, "Wow!" as he placed his king prone on the board. Lucy came running in.

"What? What are you doing? What is going on?" Lucy could see Felicity still sitting in Cliff's chair and again replacing all the pieces on the board.

"Twenty-one moves, Lucy, your little Felicity Agatha beat me in twenty-one moves!" Cliff leaned down and hugged Felicity. She did not try to move away from him.

Lucy laughed. "What do you two think you are doing?"

"No," John said. "We aren't doing anything. Felicity plays chess! Not just chess. She is good. Very, very good."

"Really?" Lucy wasn't convinced she was not being fooled by her husband and brother.

"Show me," she demanded.

"Watch," was all John said as he sat across from Felicity.

After two moves, two correct moves on Felicity's part, Lucy was stunned. When Felicity beat John again, this time in thirty-one moves, Lucy was in awe. Tears were flowing down her face.

After that they would find Felicity in her chair with the chess pieces ready to go. She would play whenever anyone would play with her. Even Lucy learned the basic moves for each piece, but she never beat Felicity, never even came close.

8.

"How long has she been at it?" Cliff asked.

"Over two hours. Since you got her that game, she is like a chess zombie. And I don't think she loses." Lucy was referring to a hand-held computerized electronic chess game that Cliff had brought home to Felicity some days ago. After letting her watch him playing three games, he had handed it to Felicity. She learned it quickly.

Some weeks later in checking the scoring history on the game screen, Cliff saw that early on Felicity had tied one game. Since then, there were no more draws. She had won every game.

9.

"Lucy." Cliff was apprehensive. "Don't get mad at me.""

"What have you done now? What did you buy? What did you do? Are you going to have to bring me some flowers, again?"

"Nothing, really."

"Tell me about the nothing."

"You know Radoslav Kolenda? The chess grandmaster?"

"Sure," said Lucy, "Everyone in town knows about him. Some folks have actually met him. He grew up here. His mom has lived here all her life."

"Well, he's coming here to visit her and Elizabeth Marie over at the pregnancy center has gotten him to agree to play chess, with any and everyone who wants to play, all comers. You know, when they go around a room and beat twenty or so players in two hours, no sweat for a grandmaster. Elizabeth is going to have each player donate $100 to the center for the honor of having Radoslav beat them."

"And?" Lucy did not want to say what she knew was coming.

"So I signed up."

"Great. That's $100 will fly out the window. What makes you think you will even get to ten moves?"

Cliff was quiet. Then he spoke.

"Not me. I signed up Felicity."

Lucy laughed out loud. Then she thought. "You know, maybe not a bad idea. Maybe she would like it. She likes chess as much as one of us holding her and singing lullabies. Why not?"

"Really?" Cliff was surprised. "I was so sure you were gonna chew on me about this one."

"No. You didn't break anything or hit anything or wreck anything or say something utterly dumb. I think Felicity might just enjoy this."

10.

The hall was not that crowded. There were 16 tables around the room, each with a chess board. Players were already seated at most of them, waiting for the grandmaster to begin. Cliff saw Elizabeth across the room.

"Cliff, this is Radoslav Kolenda."

Cliff extended his hand. "Cliff Bright. I've known your mother, Mary, all my life. She is a gem."

"So pleased to meet you."

Radoslav Kolenda had the reputation as one of the "gentlemen of chess."

"Yes, my gem. Why I come back here whenever I can."

"Your mother used to love to watch baseball, especially the New York Yankees. She got all us boys there watching them with her. And if anyone hit a home run for the Yankess, each of us got a pint of sherbet, a pint!"

"Yes, she loved her Yankees. What an interesting way of fostering that love." Radoslav glanced over at Felicity and Lucy. "Elizabeth has told me you have a very special little girl, and she plays chess."

"Yes, so special, and yes, she doesn't just play, she loves chess."

A local reporter, Carol Alexander, who had been talking to one of the men who had signed up to play, overheard the conversation.

"Can I ask you some questions?"

Cliff and Radoslav turned to her and said, in unison, "Yes," then both laughed.

"Your little girl is so special," Carol said addressing Cliff.

He interrupted her, not letting her ask a question. "Yes, for a child this age to play chess at this level is special."

Carol did not know what to say.

"I am sorry," Cliff laughed at Carol's unease." I know what you meant. Yes, Felcity Agatha is special. Down Syndrome, the kind they call 'full copy,' and then the change after the vaccines. Some want to call this 'autism' in her, but the jury is still out. I agree with your word. Whatever this is, she is special."

Cliff looked over at Lucy and Felicity as Lucy led her 'special' daughter to a place at one of the tables. She would be player number seven.

"That's our girl," Cliff said, "Just turned five years old."

Carol turned to Radoslav. "Mr. Kolenda, you are our town's only grandmaster in history. One of only two ever to come from our state. What exactly is a 'grandmaster'."

"That's a title FIDE, the world chess organization, Federation Internationale des Echecs or World Chess Federation, awards to the very best chess players. Other than 'world champion,' it is the highest ranking for a chess player. They have some very stringent rules and standards that must be met before a man or a woman can be called 'grandmaster'. "

"How long have you been one?" Carol asked.

"Since I was twenty six," Radoslav replied. "That's the case with most of us. It seems there is something about young people's brains and surging brain development before one is about twenty-five. I know I have declined somewhat since then."

"But not so much that you cannot do exhibitions like this one."

"Yes, but now and then some little surprise brings you back down to earth. Even at an event like this. I find it invigorating each time I begin. You never know."

"So you can't be demoted? Lose the title?" Carol asked.

"No, thank goodness, you are a grandmaster for life. And I suppose you hardly ever lose at events like this one?"

Radoslav smiled. "There is always the possibility of what I said 'little surprises.' Like Felicity Agatha over there. She has lucky number seven. It is my good fortune today to meet her and to play her."

A bell rang. Elizabeth spoke to everyone.

"All the non-players, please come over here to this end of the hall and we will begin the games."

Everyone except Radoslav and the players moved away from the tables. Carol and a cameraman from a local television station went to a corner from which they could view all the tables.

Felicity focused on the board and waited as Radoslav began his circuit around the room. He let each player choose black or white. He waited a few moments and then began going from table to table, responding with ease to every move.

When he got to table number seven, he saw that Felicity had chosen the black pieces. He moved a pawn to the center of the board and almost instantly Felicity moved a knight from the other side.

In reply to Felicity's fast play, instead of moving on, Radoslav looked at the board and moved another pawn to the center. Felicity immediately moved a pawn on the board's edge opposite the side of the knight.

Radoslav tried to remember. *I don't know if I have ever seen such a fast opening, ever in competition, and that opening.* As he moved on from table to table, responding quickly to each player's efforts, he could not stop thinking about table number seven and what Felicity had done. When he got back to her, he paused. After pondering what this little girl could possibly know, he made his move. Again, Felicity made her move in reply almost instantly. Radoslav stood back from the table, deep in thought. Felicity remained, as always, staring at the chess pieces.

After another fifteen or so circuits of all the tables, Radoslav had already eliminated all of his opponents, except for one man and Felicity. Each time he came to table number seven, he spent more time there than at all the other tables combined.

This was not lost on Carol and the film crew. The television cameraman had been filming each time Radoslav was at her table. Finally, Felicity was the only player left.

Carol was speaking softly into the camera, "She has just made another of her lightning fast moves." Then the camera moved from her to focus on Radoslav and the little girl at table number seven.

"Get it all. Keep filming. Keep the board in the frame," Carol told the cameraman. "Then alternate close ups of each of them."

People were steadily entering the hall to watch the little girl play chess. It was all very quiet.

This child is pure genius, he thought. Radolsav's mind was reeling with all the combinations her moves threw at him. He had not expected this as part of his visit home. He was actually enjoying it. *Now thou dost dismiss they servant in peace, O Lord,* he whispered to himself as he studied Felicity's last move.

Half an hour later Radoslav stared at the board. He made another move.

Felicity did not react with her usual speed. For some time she simply looked at the board, her head and her eyes immobile. Then she moved a rook one space.

Radoslav started to move a bishop, but then he withdrew his hand without touching it. *Astounding!* he thought. He saw it. Felicity mates in six moves.

Toppling his king over, he said, "You are full of wonder, little lady!"

Felicity sat motionless.

The crowd erupted in applause.

Felicity was till staring at the board. As the clapping continued, Cliff came up and spoke to Radoslav.

"She wants you to play it out. That is how she does it. She plays to the last move. Then she will want your king to fall only at the very end, in checkmate."

Radolsav bowed courteously to Felicity. "My little lady, as you wish."

As the cameraman continued filming, Carol smiled. *Yes, as you wish,* she thought to herself.

The crowd, now twice as large as when the event began, was again silent. Uprighting his king, Radoslav made a move. Felicity responded with her usual speed. Five moves later, he again toppled his king, stepped back and bowed to Felicity. She did not even look up. The crowd again burst into roaring applause.

"Got that? Got it all?" Carol asked the cameraman.

Grinning from ear to ear, he said, "Yes, ma'am, and we're going viral before you know it."

In all the excitement, Carol pushed her way over to Radoslav who was still standing near table seven.

"Mr. Kolenda, what just happened ?" Carol thrust the microphone in front of him.

"Rarely the world is blest with a Jesse Owens, or an Einstein, or a Jenny Lind, a Cassius Clay, a Marie Curie, a Mozart. Our world has been blest by God with this beautiful child. Yes, she is indeed the Little Lady of chess. She is a tiny lioness, and she will roar. It is God's gift to me that I was privileged to be here with her today."

Lucy went over to the table. Felicity had already arranged the pieces for another game.

"Darling, that's all there is here today. You can play with daddy when we get home."

Felicity rose from her chair, walked over to Radoslav, and stood in front of him, looking straight at him without making a sound.

"I think she is saying 'thank you,'" said Cliff.

Again, Radoslav bowed. "May I take her hand?" he asked Lucy.

"Yes, if she will let you."

Radoslav reached out slowly and grasped Felicity's hand. Then he bowed and kissed it. "I thank you, my little lady of chess."

"Got it?" Carol wanted to make sure the cameraman had not stopped filming.

By the next morning, the match and the 'Little Lady of Chess' were international news. The video of the match edited from the full tape, the extended version, and the sheet listing all the moves had over seventeen million views in less than two days. In a week, it was over sixty million.

11.

None of the three doctors were smiling. They each had a stack of papers and files in front of them on the conference table. Cliff and Lucy came in with Felicity. Felicity was totally engaged with a new chess game on a tablet computer. Dr. Carol Yarl, began.

"First, we want you to know that all of this is being funded by numerous persons and entities who have taken an interest in Felicity. She has become quite the instant international celebrity."

Cliff replied. "We had no idea how big chess is around the world. We heard from one grandmaster and let him come visit. She beat him in an impromptu game in thirty-three moves. Then came the deluge. Everyone wants to see her play. Everyone wants to play her. I guess we're glad," he continued, looking at Lucy, "because this means you are doing all this research that might help her and maybe others."

"That's our hope," said another of the doctors, doctor Bomtuan Chan. "'You know all the tests and studies and lab work and scans we have done." He looked down at the mass of papers and files on the table in front of them.

The tests and scans had included hair analysis; numerous blood tests; tissue tests and studies; radiography, both projection and fluoroscopy; MRI, tomographic magnetic resonance imaging; medical ultrasonography; elastography; photoacoustic imaging; echocardiography; encephalograms; electron microscopy; spectroscopy; other types of tomography, X-ray computed tomography (CT), computed axial tomography (CAT), and positron emission tomography (PET); and MPI, magnetic particle imaging.

The third doctor, doctor Phillipa Tracico, spoke. "This seems like a lot and it looks like there is a ton of data and results here," she motioned to all the report," but fact is, other than telling you some of the things that are present in Felicity's body, in her blood, and in her brain, we cannot tell you what is happening, or why. We also have found that there are some substances, some elements that are inexplicable."

"What do you mean?" asked Cliff.

"For example," said Doctor Yarl, "There is carbon and iron throughout her brain. We don't know its source or how it got there. And there is aluminum."

"And you have no treatment? No cure?" interjected Lucy.

The doctors looked at each other in silence. Doctor Chan replied.

"We have more to do, but for now, we have no treatment. We are on completely new ground here. Frankly, we are facing something none of us, and none of our colleagues, has ever seen. And the astounding mental abilities are, to put it bluntly, incredibly amazing to all of us. Given the facts as known now, with no information about Felicity and her history, most of us would have expected that she would be in a deep coma, or worse. But we are not giving up."

"Thank you," Lucy said. "You know, in many ways we are blest. Like you said, Doctor Chan, she is not in a coma and we know she hears us. And she still lets us hug and kiss her."

All three doctors smiled. "We will carry on," said doctor Tracico."

"Yes," said doctor Yarl, "and we will not give up."

After Cliff and Lucy had gone, doctor Tracico turned to the others and said, "Hey, what about Alexis Zarkov ?"

The other two doctors laughed out loud. Then doctor Yarl said, "What have we got to lose? Someone needs to look at this all differently, someone needs to start thinking outside the box, for Felicity."

12.

Doctor Alexis Hans Zarkov worked alone. He preferred it that way. Degrees in chemistry and engineering, medical doctor, doctorate in bioengineering, nanorobot designer for intracorporeal delivery, and, as many considered him, a genius geek. He had heard of this incredibly young chess prodigy, the assumed autism diagnosis, the Down Syndrome, and then he saw pictures of Felicity, pre-two-years old and after. He printed them out and put them on the wall by his desk.

Doctor Yarl called.

"Felicity Bright? Yes, I have heard of her. Have her photo right here. Very interesting case."

Dr. Yarl was surprised Dr. Zarkov knew anything about Felicity. "Do you have any interest in reviewing all the files and all the tests. We are at dead ends."

Dr. Zarkov's brain started going and as had happened so many times in the past, he could not stop it. After the information was sent to him he began waking every day at 4 a.m. or earlier thinking about Felicity.

They said he either thought outside the box or tore it into kindling for his imagination's fire. That was how he envisioned and then made the first working prototype for the Moebius circuit and its infinite storage capacity. All dreams. No one had ever been able to make one, but to him it seemed to make sense.

He read and re-read everything about Felicity, all the data, all the tests, four or five times, and let it all roll around in his head for a week or so. He started on the internet, general searches, rabbit trails, apparently disconnected facts, looking for any data or information that had not been noticed or taken into account.

Then he pulled up Cliff's curriculum vitae and resume associated with a press release for a new nanotech company with which Cliff had consulted.

"Bingo!" he yelled.

"Hey," it's Alexis." Doctor Zarkov was calling doctor Tracico. "Please, run two more tests, one FNIR imaging, one confocal laser endomicroscopy."

"Do you know what this little girl has been through?" Phillipa asked.

"I know. Read it all. All of it, several times. But please. I think something has been missed. Please."

"I will call her parents. At the beginning they were 'full speed ahead,' but now as we have tested, and poked, and prodded, and tested and scanned and re-tested Felicity, they wonder if there is any point."

"Great. Please ask. And in all you sent, I did not get the magnetic particle imaging results. Need that too."

"On its way, Alexis Hans," Phillipa said, shaking her head.

"One more thing," added Alexis.

Oh, no thought Phillipa.

"Can you make it a whole-body FNIR?"

Phillipa had never heard of anyone doing this. She thought for some moments.

"You still there?" Alexis asked.

"Yes. We'll see. I don't see any reason why not."

13.

All on her own, Felicity Agatha Bright, the Little Lady of Chess, had rejuvenated interest in chess worldwide. This was not lost on the FIDE officers and executives.

What a young man named "Cassius Marcellus Clay" had done for boxing in the 1960s, this Little Lady had done for chess, almost overnight. What had happened was more dramatic than Bobby Fischer's accomplishments for chess in the 1960s and 1970s. Bobby Fischer beat many grandmasters, becoming a grandmaster himself at the age of 15, and winning the world championship at the age of 29.

As quickly as it could be scheduled and set up, a FIDE event was arranged in the city, forty miles from Felicity's home. It would be a fully sanctioned event, with points counting toward rankings and for grandmaster status.

Many grandmasters did not want to take part for fear of losing, and then be listed among those defeated by a little five-year-old girl. Four of them, however, were eager to challenge this mere child, this chess prodigy. The event would follow a one-loss elimination format with a draw eliminating neither player.

The current world champion, grandmaster Robert John Piscator, could not change his scheduled appearances and events, but he did send his best wishes to all the contestants and a, "You go, girl," on social media addressed to "FAB, The Little Lady of Chess."

Cliff saw Felicity sit down for the first game across from one of the grandmaster opponents. Then he saw something he had not noticed, something he had not seen since Felicity was a small child.

He thought back to how she had begun to speak, clearly at four months, and then by six months she was saying night prayers. Felicity always put her hands together and bowed her head. Cliff rememberd the words of the prayer.

He and Lucy would begin and Felicity would repeat a line at a time.

"Infant Jesus, meek and mild."

"Inpan Gigi, meekamild."

"Pity me, a little child."

"Pitta me a lil child."

"Infant Jesus, all I do,"

"Inpan Gigi, alla do,"

"I do if for the love of You."

" Ah do if for luvva You."

"God bless mommy and daddy and my grandpas and grandmas and everyone."

"God bless mommydaddy and grandies mamaws."

In the hall for the event, Cliff said, "Lucy," to get her attention. Then pointed to Felicity. Cliff was certain he saw Felicity put her hands together and bow her head before she again looked up at the chess board. Lucy recognized immediately what Felicity was doing.

"Yes. Yes," said Lucy. "She is still our Felicity."

14.

Each of Felicity's games turned out to be a classic. She beat her first opponent in 37 moves, leaving four other players, when two of them had played to a first round draw. In the next round, the highest ranking grandmaster, Samuel Maccabeus, who had set out the first round, played one of the players who had drawn that first game. Samuel won.

Felicity played, and, in 39 moves beat the other grandmaster who had achieved the first round draw. That left her and Samuel to play each other.

Lucy walked with Felicity to the game table and then came across the room and stood by Cliff. They both watched as Felicity again put her hands together and bowed her head.

"I am not imagining this," Cliff told Lucy.

"Our Felicity is praying." Lucy smiled and there were tears in her eyes.

Then, as usual, Felicity sat up and began staring intently at the board before her first move. As she had with Radoslav, she began with a knight and then moved a pawn on the other side of the board. This opening was now being called the "Little Lady Gambit." 19 moves later she beat Samuel.

He was gracious, even happy.

"This is chess brilliancy," said a beaming Samuel. "The likes of which I have not seen since Bobby Fischer's 21-move brilliancy masterpiece, the 'greatest game ever played,' against Robert Byrne in 1963. I do not know if anyone in the world right now could beat this Little Lady."

15.

They were all, all 22 of them, like well-paid mercenary soldiers being sent on a no-return impossible mission into enemy territory against overwhelming odds. There were no smiles.

Gesta Sanger, who evidently was in charge, spoke when they had all been seated around a long table in the large conference room.

"We are meeting here for obvious reasons. And, as far as each of you is concerned, as we have in the past, there is no meeting today. You are not here. No notes. No texts. No emails. No recordings. No records. Please, for now, turn off all your computers, all your devices, and all your phones."

Gesta was referring to all the work they had done for over 20 years now, none of it even remotely traceable to the entities who hired them, entities known to those in the room, and in no known way related to anything they had ever done. The entities unnamed, the companies never mentioned. She did not tell them that electronic jammers were, at that moment, preventing any wireless communications into or out of the room.

She continued. "Up until now we have done incredibly well. This is, in part, due to the fact that we have unlimited funding, which you all have enjoyed, to do what we do. It is also due to the fact that, worldwide, we have so many people in academia, so many in the concerned corporations and related industries, so many governments, their officials, and legislators working with us, so many politicians and people in power, which, of course, goes back to our funding abilities."

Heads nodded around the table.

"As you all are well aware, we have, in essence, paid for luxury automobiles, exquisite jewelry, rare artworks, retirement plans, children's education, mistresses and consorts, pleasures upon pleasures, homes and vacation homes around the world for those who help us. Which brings me to the point of this meeting today, this meeting that is not occurring."

Most of the people sitting around the table had their suspicions about why the meeting had been called. Most of them were correct.

Gesta had laughed out loud when she came up with the name 'mogul' for the heads of the various divisions. Now the moguls for all of them, and their upper 'minions' as Gesta defined them, were present. She could not remember when all of them had ever been assembled together at one time; all of them present – print-books; print-periodicals; online; legislation-state; legislation-federal; legislation-local; social media; radio – network, cable and internet; television-network;

television-cable; television-internet; academia; independent research; lawsuit-monitoring; and lawsuit-intervention.

"Until now, it really has been relatively easy to not only control all the information and control the narrative, that we have come to call the 'goodness story,' but to make it part not just of news, but part of the very fabric of societies around the world. Vaccines are safe, vaccines are good, good for all of us, good for the 'common good.' And good people care about the common good.   They haven't even figured out we are "imposing a morality" on them. Yes, there might be here and there some minor complications, some temporary condition, but none directly related to the life-giving, life-protecting vaccines. All there is is safe, safe, safe and good, good, good,"

Many people sitting around the table, knowing what had been done for over two decades, smiled. They knew the successes they had had, which they had engineered, which they had brought into being like reality magicians.

"I said 'until now.' Until now we have never had to face anything like this little girl." Gesta proceeded, almost with a sneer, "the 'Little Lady Of Chess.' "

A slide appeared on a large screen in the room. It was a picture of Felciity sitting at a chess table across from a grandmaster.

"You have all heard about her. Idiosavant, genius, prodigy, freak, human computer, miracle, darling little Down Syndrome creature, autistic victim - whatever. And practically every story and every blog and every interview and every article mentions the alleged fact that normal, good vaccines were the trigger, the cause for her 'condition'. We have never dealt with something like this. Did you know they play chess everywhere? There is no language barrier. Just a board, the chess men, and two people. They don't even have to speak the same language. All around the world!"

Margaret Slee, mogul for social media, raised her hand. "But we have dealt with similar things, for Big Soda, Big Sugar, and Big Pharma before. And some of us here are old enough to remember in the early days what we accomplished for Big Fluoride and Big Tobacco. With unbelievable success. Tell me, has tobacco been outlawed? Anyone ever go to jail for fluoridating water in Poughkeepsie? And tobacco. With all the lost lawsuits, all the cancer deaths, all the emphysema suffering, all the 'health' warnings, all the family members still alive? Tobacco prohibited? Been to your grocery store lately? No way. Actually, there are selling some kinds of tobacco today at record profits, more than in all our history – with tons of taxes to governments at all levels."

Yes," replied Gesta, "But never has there been someone like this little girl, 'FAB' they call her. No cancer victim of first or second-hand tobacco smoker ever achieved world class status at tennis. No sugar-addict diabetic with legs amputated has ever run in the Olympics. No one who committed suicide after two doses of SeisTreble miracle depression drug has ever made international news for achieving anything. No, this is different, and how we negate her and nullify the effects of what she has done and what she continues to do will also have to be different."

"So, why this, why now, so what if she is a sensation? asked Lilith Steiner, the mogul for print-periodicals.

"You all know, better than most in this country, money talks and baloney walks. Couple that with the first principle of explaining human endeavor, 'Follow The Money,' and you will understand why we are here. For decades, there have been annual standing orders for vaccines, for hundreds of millions and some billions of dollars, most of them with a plus factor for the inevitable periodic population increases for countries worldwide, despite any reductions due to the use of vaccines. "

"So is anyone canceling their orders? "asked Lilith.

"Not yet. But some current, valid standing orders have been 'postponed' and many countries and governments have put a hold on the automatic renewal of orders. They have stock piling up in storage, unused, because parents worldwide have seen this Little Lady and heard her story. And even with the metal preservatives, that storage, month after month, gets to be prohibitively expensive. And then either out-of-date vaccines are used, they are destroyed, or sold on the dark market, some for repackaging. All of which means no new orders. Government after government is saying they just can't free up the money right now to pay for orders already filled and shipped."

The mogul of academic liaisons, Louise Higgins, spoke. "She is friggin' adorable. Have you watched her? Now they say she prays. Prays to her freakin' God. She is known around the world. She has no record of ever doing anything wrong. She is five! Five years old! And we cannot implicate her in any of the usual drunk driving, affairs, corruption, perversions, cooked-up assaults, kickbacks, dirty money, hate speech, nepotism, and crimes. She is a true untouchable, seems unstoppable, along with all the bad press for vaccines."

Gesta spoke again. "We have a plan. For beginners, we are gathering every bit of information on her parents and her grandparents. And her extended family. Seems there are one huge bunch of them. She has over 140, really, over 140 cousins. Who are these people? Don't they know what causes this? Ever hear of condoms? We also have a strategy much like those in the past that includes ongoing, daily, detailed monitoring of all information sources, news, online media, print, radio and television. And all our blog and comment trolls. Of course we have our people, or those they influence, in all of these."

"How do we deny the truth this time?" asked Barry Tesora, mogul of all online monitoring and response.

"What does a criminal defense attorney do when all the evidence points to his client being the murderer?" Gesta asked. "He gives the jury another killer. Actually, just the possibility of another killer will do. Keep in mind what we always say, there is no 'scientific' proof that her vaccines caused her condition. Science has become the peoples' new religion. Keep in mind all the other possible causes we have dreamed up for decades. How do you think the people were fooled about smoking for so long? Hard to believe the ads and commercials years ago that touted tobacco as a health benefit. There are several other possible causes for lung cancer, for emphysema. And never forget 'well, she just had bad genes' ploy. Why do you think so many foods today still have gobs of sugar in them, with the over 100 names we have invented for it? Sugar is not only 'natural,' diabetes has many causes."

Barry Tesora interrupted. "And no new parent wants anyone to think they are stupid or they don't love their child."

"Spot on," said Gesta, "and that's why long ago we put the subtle message out that only lower class mamas and daddies failed to have their children vaccinated. People who have trusted, who have taken vaccines time-out-of-mind and had their children do so, do not want to think they have been as stupid as trailer trash. They sure don't want to look dumb to their other family members and friends. So we give them another suspect, and they happily continue getting the vaccines. This strategy worked for decades with smoking. It's working with sugar. And it is working with vaccines- that is, until now – until this 'Little Lady' showed up."

Barry asked another question. "What about all the reports, that sound true, of parents going in, kids get vaccines, kids end up autistic, brain damaged, or dead?"

Gesta smirked. "Barry, aren't you the one years back who told us about that wonderful word, 'anecdotal'? All those personal stories are just stories. Call them 'anecdotal' and add 'but science says . . .' and the general public thinks those parents are mistaken, there is no 'scientific proof', or those mommies and daddies are lying to back up a baseless legal claim. Never mind that we gutted the monetary motive to sue, that they usually cannot file a lawsuit for the child's injuries or death."

Gesta was referring to the National Vaccine Injury Compensation Program and the individuals who had filed a petition with the government for compensation for injury due to a vaccine. This prohibited most typical personal injury lawsuits. Since the program began, over $4 billion had been paid for these claims. In many cases, because of this program, by law, makers and sellers of vaccines had been shielded from lawsuits alleging harm or injury, or death, caused by a vaccine.

Gesta continued. "So, everyone is to go on as we usually do, but now we have a new task. We have to turn all these negative stories around, come up with a positive reply. Commercials with healthy, happy babies. Focus on the good for everyone when everyone is vaccinated, and the risk level so low that it really doesn't matter. Human interest reports with mommies and daddies smiling, and hugging their vaccinated babies. Proactive, positive. Back here in two weeks with all your ideas."

"And how do we deal with those who make a point of the irony, some say hypocrisy," aske Margaret Slee, "of how we have used the 'my-body-my-self' mantra for "choice," but we don't want anyone to have any free choice about vaccines? Aren't there still about 17 states where people, parents are free to opt out of getting kids vaccinated? How do we deal with that?"

Gesta and everyone else in the room were silent.

"That's another thing to put on our agenda for next time." Gesta began to pick up her papers and her laptop. The meeting was over.

16.

"Sorry I'm late."

No one around the table said a word. Felicity, sitting between Cliff and Lucy stared at the ceiling and then at the wall on the far side of the room. The other doctors were waiting to see what doctor Zarkov had to say.

He walked around the table and extended his hand to Cliff.

"Hello, I am Alexis Zarkov." Then he shook Lucy's hand. She held his hand for some moments and then let go.

"It's good to meet you," Lucy said. "They told us you may have discovered something."

Felicity turned, almost imperceptibly, and looked in doctor Zarkov's general direction. "I'm Alexis Zarkov," he said, standing by Felicity. She continued to stare straight ahead. He walked back to all the materials and papers he had brought into the room.

"Well, let's see what I've been thinking about." He pointed to a slide that had now appeared on a nearby screen. "What you see on the screen are the results one of the first tests of Felicity and then with the magnetic particle imaging for Felicity's whole body overlaid over that." The projected image looked like the outline of Felicity's body with some fairly clear definition. Felicity had turned to look at the screen. She seemed to be paying attention to the presentation.

"Now, I noticed that you, Cliff, worked with a company doing research on delivery of various substances into human bodies using carbon nanotubes. We call them 'CNTs.' With all this in its infancy, I know that there is no way that they had in place what is needed so that you were not adversely exposed to the CNTs. No matter what they do now, ventilation, face filters, gloves, storage, masks, suits, isolation, and inventory controls, the whole nine-yards, they don't yet know how to deal with these things. And you were in contact with them. Literally contacting them."

"That is spot on," Cliff said. "They followed all the regulations and protocols, but I see what you are saying. Due to the nature of this stuff, I agree with you. There is no way I was not exposed to the CNTs and, most probably, I had them on my skin and clothes, and even could have breathed them in."

Carbon nanotubes are incredibly tiny, highly organized pieces of carbon, small little cylinders. They are so small you could put 50,000 of them side-by-side on one human hair. Decades ago they were not widely available, and they were super expensive, beyond price. Since then technological developments have made them relatively cheap, with some companies selling them by the ounce or by the pound. Ongoing research was trying to determine if they could pass through the blood-brain barrier.

"And you worked with some that were functionalized with iron."

Functionalized nanotubes have some other element besides carbon bonded to them, atoms or molecules, and this changes the chemical properties of the nanotube.

"You are correct," said Cliff. "And I never thought twice about it or worried that me or my family could be hurt by them."

"You probably didn't even know you brought them home. Tiny, Inert, virtually invisible to the naked eye when not present in large masses or in a glass container. Well, with that in mind, I thought it would be interesting to see if Felicity had ingested any of them. Here are some curious results for the tests that they had already done and from what I asked for."

Doctor Zarkov showed another slide, this time with the results of the FNIR testing. Then he said, "Now, let's overlay that on the other two slides." A startling image of Felicity's entire body appeared.

"But there's more!" said doctor Zarkov. Then he had a slide overlaid on all of them with the results of the laser endomicroscopy.

"No way!" said doctor Phillipa.

"Wow!" was all that doctor Carol said.

"This is marvelous, amazing," said doctor Bomtuan Chan.

The image looked like a human body with an interior network from head to toe of lattice-like structures, many interconnected, many adjacent each other.

"I believe what you are seeing is two things," said doctor Zarkov. First, there is the interstitium and then there is this net-like reticulated structure that extends almost everywhere in the Felicity's interstitium, and beyond in several locations. And there are these lattice structures in her blood system, and in her lymph system, but not all connected. Still close enough that there may be communication. And they are in her. Everywhere."

"Interstitium?" asked Cliff.

"It's a fluid-filled space that covers the body under the skin. Some want to call it a newly discovered organ, some don't. I guess some of these M Deities think they look stupid for missing this one for about two thousand years. Whatever you call it, it is there. And you can see Felicity's," he pointed to the screen. "And you can see it contains this network. You can also, if you look here," he pointed to the brain, "that these structures cross the blood-brain barrier."

"What does that all mean?" asked Lucy.

Felicity continued to stare at the screen.

"The test results say this latticework is made up of carbon, iron and aluminum. And there is something else, within spaces within some of the structures. I think the carbon and iron are from the functionalized CNTs Cliff was exposed to. I think the aluminum is from some of the vaccines Felicity got, and maybe some of it from you, Mrs. Bright."

"How does this explain anything?" asked Cliff. "And what can we do?"

Doctors Yarl, Chan and Tracico were silent. Doctor Zarkov continued.

"This is what I think," he said. "Keep in mind, this is just me. I have never seen anything like this and never heard of any work or research on this. Also keep in mind, carbon nanotubes are a better conductor of electricity than copper. Copper, the usual standard for electrical conductivity, is rated at 100%. Carbon can do much better than that, easily twice as good, in some cases up to a hundred times better, or more. Keep in mind that for some time it has been accepted that the gut is a human being's 'second brain. "

"My stomach is a brain?" interrupted Cliff.

"Well, not like that. Here's what I see. You've got to quit thinking of the body as this part connected to this other separate part which itself is connected to this other independent part, like the railcars on a train or separate dominoes in a row. It's one totally interconnected and responsive system. The body train is all one, the locomotive, the cars, the caboose, all of it, one big single vehicle. And it is not only the brain cells inside the skull that 'think' as we have believed all these years. The body's thinking system is much more, maybe all that you see here interconnected, all this that has all this carbon-iron lattice work running through it. Her brain hemispheres, connected and communicating. The lobes of her brain, in direct communication, connected, included. Her toes and fingertips like her eyes, directly connected via all this to the brain. In a nutshell, *all* of this is Felicity's thinking system, her brain and all that is now in communication with it, and she is using all of it, or a lot of it, much more than usual, since it is now connected in this way, to do what she does."

"How?" was all Cliff could say.

"We don't know, said doctor Zarkov. "I have read about some new research that says that nanotubes can be used as infinitesimally small needles to go through a cell wall and to put material inside a cell. Something no one has ever done before. This research indicates that it may be possible to change genes with these tiny 'needles.' If that can be done, the sky is the limit for editing, changing, a gene. And some of your CNTs, Cliff, may be what we see here that appears to cross cell and brain barriers. Or they provide the pathway for this for other materials."

Lucy looked at the other three doctors. "What do you think?"

None of them wanted to reply. Finally doctor Chan spoke. "I think I speak for all of us. This is a very interesting theory. We don't know what to think. Before today we have never seen or heard anything like this. If this is true, we are going to need a new paradigm for human thought. And for explaning your phenomenal child. A 'Felicity Paradigm'."

"There is one more thing."

All eyes turned back to doctor Zarkov.

"In a typical electrical circuit you see wires, lines, single pathways, multiple branching lines, from here to there, sometimes multiple ones in series or parallel. One path, electrons in, electrons out, or clearly defined pathways. Some years ago I hypothesized that there could be a circuit with an endless structure, like in a Moebius loop. With infinite capacity to retain information. I called it a 'Moebius Circuit'."

Doctor Zarkov put up a new slide with an artist's rendition of what he had envisioned.

"Never could figure out how to make one, no one else could, but all the theory and all the math seemed right. Nobody really challenged me. Just said to let them know when I made one. Now, look at this."

A new slide appeared with part of Felicity's interstitium lattice work enlarged.

"These CNTs are circular, cylinders. These are called 'MWNTs' or multi-walled nanotubes, cylinders within cylinders. And some of them are located and connected so that a signal, electrical signal, or a current, electrical current flowing to them could traverse around one or both cylinders again and again, maybe from one cylinder to the other and then back, maybe again and again, before exiting the CNT structure and going to the next one. Each time around either cylinder could constitute one signal. Each time around, a new signal. This would not be what we call 'linear transmission.' I am calling it 'Moebius Transmission.' And it could account for the apparent incredible and limitless capacity of Felicity for seeing endless possibilities and for her unbelievable speed in making responsive moves during a chess game."

The room was quiet.

"So," Cliff's voice broke the silence. "If this is all true, what can be done?"

Doctor Zarkov shook his head. I am sorry, but anything we would come up with would be totally new, totally experimental, and without question almost certainly with risk to Felicity. Immediately, you think of taking the bad stuff out. I have thought of one thing, but it seemed to me it most likely would be incredibly dangerous, or worse. Lab animals, fine. Your beautiful daughter, no."

Felicity seemed to be taking this all in. She stared intently at each new slide on the screen.

"What is it?" Cliff could not refrain from asking.

"Some years ago some researchers were thinking about what happened to astronauts in space, and in particular to their blood in space, with all the gamma rays, solar radiation, and the incredibly confined environment of a space shuttle, a pressurized capsule, or of an orbiting lab or station with all that was floating around in there with no place to go. The astronauts were not only exposed to whatever, but probably taking some of it in, breathing and through their eyes and skin. Of all the things they came up with, one was a way to take the blood out of an astronaut, treat it, clean it, and then return it back to the same astronaut. They called it ECAB treatment, 'extracorporeal autologous blood' treatment. This included methods for removing specified things or particles from blood."

Everyone in the room listened without comment. Doctor Zarkov went on.

"What I see in this latticework in Felicity's body are some very specific building blocks, made of very specific materials. So far it looks like primarily carbon, iron and aluminum. Luckily they are all bound together, so if you can get the iron out, you could get the carbon, and maybe the aluminum, along with it. Or break the bonds, maybe with specific enzymes, and then remove the pieces, the individual molecules."

Doctor Tracico interrupted. "How?"

"My dreams haven't gone much further yet than thinking about the iron, and enzymes, and chelation. And magnets used outside Felicity's body focused on the interstitium fluid and the blood and strong enough and near enough to attract the iron. They could be powerful hard magnets or electromagnets, or both. Also, I think there is an enzyme that could break the aluminum bonding. Whether or not to impose an electric current across the blood and fluid during all this, I haven't pursued very much. And then there are the tiny CNT tunnels that are everywhere. In theory, metal molecules could be removed through those tunnels."

"Dreams?" asked doctor Yarl.

"Well, a little more than dreams," said doctor Zarkov as he put up another slide on the screen with a rough drawing of a system adjacent the depiction of Felicity's body and extracorporeal systems for blood and for fluid from the interstitium, with some magnets, enzyme inputs, chelator inputs, drains, and electric current devices.

Doctor Chan studied the slide. "And because these CNTs can traverse the blood-brain barrier, and there is a pathway through the nanotubes, either with one pass or multiple passes, you will actually remove material from inside her brain? From intracranial neurons, synapses? From cells?"

"I don't know. I just don't know. This idea just came up this morning. I haven't really worked it out much beyond what you see and what I have said. There could to be some way to break some of the bonds in the lattice. Maybe enzymes. Maybe microwaves. Still thinking about that one. One way to remove things from the blood is called 'chelation,' usually done inside a person's body. Used for decades to treat lead poisoning and other metal poisoning. Once we have access to it outside Felicity's body we could do a chelation process. Chelation is used successfully for the treatment of heavy metal poisoning. The 'chelate,' a chemical substance, attaches or binds to the heavy metal you want to remove. Here's a list of what can be removed and another list of how chelation has been used."

Doctor Bomtuan Chan was curious. "I see the autologous blood system, and these exist and are used very day. But I don't see how you can, basically, drain off part of the interstitium and then put it back in. I don't see it 'flowing' like blood in what is in essence one interconnected, communicating blood system."

"Yes," replied doctor Zarkov. "I am thinking that for the interstitium fluid we stay location-specific. Take some fluid out of one body location, clean it, and put it back in the same place."

Doctor Carol Yarl was thinking out loud. "You know. We have never really explained cancer metastases. People thought lymph system, blood system, separate and isolated systems, not in fluid communication with each other. No interconnecting pathway has ever been proven. The instestitium could be the cancer cell freeway throughout the whole body. And yes, the heavy metal superhighway to the brain. Usually, all the radiation and chemotherapy we do kills cancer cells, but not cancer stem cells — and the interstitium could be how these resilient stem cells flow — metastasize — throughout the body. All very interesting. But I don't see how this could be done without harm to the patients. We could be years, if not decades, away from doing this in the real world."

"I agree," said doctor Zarkov.

He handed papers to Lucy and Cliff that listed diseases and materials and elements that could be removed by chelation, including mercury, iron, arsenic, lead, aluminum, cadmium, copper, gold, uranium, plutonium, beryllium, arsenic, tungsten, chromium, manganese, and nickel. The listed conditions and diseases included: heavy metal poisoning, autism, Parkinson's disease, Alzheimer's disease, heart disease, diabetes, atherosclerosis, aceruloplasminemia, biliary cirrhosis, Cooley's anemia (thalassemia major), cystinuria, Diamond-Blackfan anemia, secondary hemochromatosis, sickle cell anemia and Wilson's disease.

"Well, it's infinitely more than anyone has told us for some years now," said Lucy, looking at Cliff and then at Felicity.

'I see," said Cliff, "if this was done, it could all backfire and literally remove parts of Felicity's brain. And who knows what else. Am I right?"

The other three doctors shook their heads and were silent.

"I think you are right," doctor Zarkov told Cliff. "Chelation alone has resulted in death, chelation done inside the body. And I am envisaging chelation outside the body, and possibly inside also. And possibly removing material and even tissue from inside the brain. And I would not tell you to do it. If it was me and I had this all in me and someone presented this to me and I thought maybe this could fix me, I would not jump at the chance. But I might do it. Then again, the brain is too fragile, too intricate, too delicate. Despite what some M Deity may tell you, there is, for me, way too much we still do not know about the human brain. And I am sure that then I would think, and think again, about the possibility, the possibility of help versus the very real danger. And if it was my child, my Felicity, I would not know what to do. I think I would decide against it."

"Can you give us a copy of all this?" Lucy asked.

"Not only that, and hard copies, but I will also email all this and links to many of the sources I have followed up on," said doctor Zarkov.

17.

Later that week Lucy came into their dining room and saw Cliff silent, staring out the window. His laptop was on in front of him and the table and the floor around it were covered with the information, reports and discs, documents and folders, and papers, everything from doctor Zarkov and everything they had found themselves over the past several years.   Cliff turned when he heard Lucy.

"What do we do?" He handed Lucy the diagram of the system doctor Zarkov had designed. "Looks so good on paper, but this is our little girl."

"I know," said Lucy. "We are going to pray and let God take care of this. Felicity is His special child too. He holds her in the palm of His hand. He will tell us."

"You are so sure," said Cliff. "You have faith."

"Faith is not some golden glow you walk around with, Cliff Bright. It is not a godly gift He gives you and you put away in a cabinet. It is a gift that lets you act, helps you act, freely. You choose, in faith, in response to the gift. Faith is an act of the will, and you and I are going to act on this faith. You'll see. He gave us, no one else, this child, this unique little person, for a reason."

"Right now," said Cliff, "my faith is saying 'no'. "

18.

Gesta thought of the irony of her waiting, alone, in a corner lounge of the mezzanine of the Five Quarters hotel for Wilhelm Doorman, entrepreneur, billionaire, global power elite. She had heard of the man, but had never met him. Many times she had suspected that she felt his unseen hand in their work, but this had never been confirmed. She had been astounded when one of his executives had contacted her about this clandestine meeting.

The hallway was deserted. Nothing had been scheduled for these rooms for the entire week. Doorman left nothing to chance.

She saw him walking toward her with no bodyguards, no entourage, business suit, humorless, unsmiling, implacable. He did not greet her.

"She is a child, but she is unbeatable."

Doorman stared out the window.

"By a human," he said.

"Ignoring the sales figures, publicity about her has had a devastating effect on the perception, worldwide, about safety. And the lay-down-your-life-for-your-friend gambit takes on a whole new meaning when you ask a mother to lay down the life of her own child for some unknown person half way around the world, and even more so when you ask that mother to do this for the 'common good'."

Doorman was silent. He was too well aware of the unbelievableand almost instant impact this little girl had had on the bottom line of so many of his entities, and how what she was doing, despite her "adverse event," had affected the balance of power in so many countries where his people were in control. Until now.

"Can you arrange it with Azure Main?" Gesta knew the answer before she asked the question. There was very little anywhere on earth that Doorman could not 'arrange.'

"We must weigh heavily the impact of doing this at all, and of doing it publicly. Yes, she will lose, but will that help us?"

Gesta was thoughtful. "The blame-the-CNTs propaganda has not worked. People around the world believe that the toxic metals, many from preservatives, in her brain have re-wired it and morphed her into a chess genius. If we continue to do nothing, that myth will become the new paradigm. And people will believe it."

"Have her parents told that this will help spread the truth. Will help countless other little girls and little boys. I will see to it. And she will lose." Wilhelm Doorman turned and walked away.

19.

Lucy had a friend who knew a technician who worked at a chelation clinic in the city near the small town where the Brights lived. She had arranged for Lucy and Cliff to go there and meet the clinic directors and learn about the process.

"I'm doctor Alan," said the clinic's physician in charge, extending his hand to Cliff.

"I'm nurse Julie McClure," said a smiling lady with a stethoscope around her neck."

"So good of you to let us come and learn," said Lucy.

"We are happy to have you," said doctor Alan, "And, as it turns out, both myself and Jessie play chess. We have watched all the stories and news about your amazing daughter since it hit the internet. Hopefully, we can give you some useful information."

They explained the chelation process and let Lucy know that it was originally approved for treatment of acute lead poisoning and then was used to remove other heavy metals. More recently its use has been extended to treatments for other conditions and diseases. Fairly recently, medical insurance had begun to accept charges for these other conditions.

"'Chelate' means "grab," said doctor Alan. "These chelators, these 'grabbers,' are put into the bloodstream and then they latch onto the heavy metals and then help the body eliminate them. Not just heavy metals, but also some minerals, like calcium. This process has been used to remove lead, mercury, copper, iron, arsenic, aluminum, chromium, tungsten, cadmium, lead mercury, iron, copper, manganese, arsenic, nickel, silver, and beryllium."

A nurse came into the conference room and doctor Alan and nurse McClure said they had to help with a procedure, but that they would be back as soon as they could.

Lucy asked them where the ladies room was and left the conference room. When she was walking down the hallway, she saw a young woman sitting in a chair, her head in her hands. The woman looked up and Lucy could see she had been crying.

"Can I do anything ?" Lucy said.

The young woman tried to smile. "I wish you could bring me back my son, the way he was."

Lucy knelt down and put her arms around the young woman and let her cry.

"I'm Lucy. I'm here with my husband Cliff. We're trying to learn as much as we can about the procedures they do here."

This seemed to calm the young woman.

"Why are you here ?" she asked Lucy.

Lucy wondered how much she should say about Felicity and why they were learning about chelation.

"Our daughter, Felicity, had some vaccines and the next day she was different. We are trying to find out why, and if there is anything we can do."

"You are the mom of the Little Lady of Chess!" said the young woman. "I'm Bernadette. Everyone here knows about Felicity, everyone! I am so happy to meet you."

Bernadette hugged Lucy.

"We have begun to think that what happened to Felicity had something to do with what was in the vaccines."

Bernadette stopped crying. "You should know. Everyone here today, and there are three of us with our children, the oldest three years old, everyone here has a story like yours. Each of our children received a vaccine or vaccines, or multiple doses of a vaccine, and then in a short time, most of them within 72 hours or less, our children were changed. They say 'autistic' or 'ADHD,' but they should call it VS, vaccine syndrome."

"Everyone ?" asked Lucy.

"Everyone here today, all three of us. And on many days when I am here, everyone here has the same story. Others come for chelation for other reasons, but most of us who come here have a vaccine story to tell and a child still alive, but a child we have lost."

Lucy hugged Bernadette again and thanked her.

"We are trying to see if there is something that can be done for Felicity. It's not just heavy metals with her. And we are praying."

Bernadette paused. Then she spoke. "OK, we all here have the 'prayer deal' going. Everyone has agreed to pray for each of these children and for their families, daily if we can. Now we're doing the prayer deal for Felicity and you and your husband. Mommies and daddies are included."

Bernadette put her hand out to Lucy. Lucy took it and clasped both of her hands around it.

"It's a deal!" she said and then hugged Bernadette again.

20.

After sixteen moves, Azure Main had not defeated Felicity. Everybody watching was amazed. Her new nickname, "Fab, the fabulous Little Lady of Chess," was proving to be correct.

In another city, a news reporter stood in a large room with numerous computer screens, with one or two people at each screen. The reporter began looking at all the screens and then turned to the camera.

" 'Azure Main' is the computer program developed to play chess. It has now beaten twenty-one grandmasters and countless other opponents. Over fifteen years in the making, originally a team of thirty-two set out to develop the most powerful chess-playing program ever written. Over the last several years, that number has swelled to over a hundred, including chess experts, computer programmers, statisticians, mathematicians, scientists, and certified grandmasters from around the world."

The camera returned to showing all the screens and consoles and people in the room.

"The moves in the game with Felicity Bright are generated here and then transmitted almost instantaneously to the game location."

In the beginning, years back, Azure Main had lost a game here and there, and taken many others to a draw. Now, however, it was believed to be unbeatable. Capitalizing on the power and reach of the internet, and employing some neural network implementations that allowed anyone to qualify to play, Azure Main had played game after game, many hundreds of thousands, and the moves, strategy and outcome were then taken into account in the programming and in the play in each new game.

Using human terms, some said Azure Main "learned;" others said the computer was actually "thinking." It had been given the data and knew and remembered every known game of every known player, since games were first recorded to the present, from amateur to grandmaster to world champions. The history of all reported chess games was recorded, accessible, and taken into account in this program.

"Until now," the reporter continued, no one can even come close to beating this super program. In its most recent games, no one has lasted more than thirty-five moves. Most players lose in many less moves. Almost no one can play it to a draw, including grandmasters."

In effect, when you signed online to play it, you were playing many hundreds of the best chess players of all time, simultaneously. When a single grandmaster began a game, it was as if there was a crowd of other grandmasters sitting on the other side of the board. All this made Felicity's remaining in the game for some moves beyond the norm all the more astounding.

"Everyone here involved with Azure Main is confident it is simply a matter of time, and probably very little time, when the Little Lady of Chess is beaten."

21.

April 30. TNews.   Little Lady Of Chess, Champion Despite Challenges

Over the last few months five-year-old Felicity Agatha Bright has captivated the world. The lovable "Little Lady Of Chess" has stunned chess experts and grandmasters by not only beating them, but by beating them in record time, in some cases with a stunning minimal number of moves.

'FAB,' as she has become affectionately known to those who follow her story, is a Down Syndrome child. There is something else, however, that makes her accomplishments even more amazing. Unfortunately her body has been contaminated with carbon nanotubes. Although the source has not been definitely identified, her father, Cliff, did encounter the high-tech material in some of his consulting work.

Carbon nanoutbes are also called "buckytubes." They are very tiny, what is termed 'nanoscale,' little cylinders, tiny hollow tubes made of carbon atoms. You can put about 50,000 of them side by side on a single human hair. There are several kinds of these nanotubes. One of the simplest is "single walled carbon nanotubes, or SWNTs.

SWNTs come in various forms themselves. Three primary types of SWNTs have been discovered, named "zigzag," "armchair," and "chiral." These structural variations result in differences in electrical conductivity and mechanical strength.

In his work, Felicity's father encountered the single-walled form and also a somewhat more complex form called "multiple walled" carbon nanotubes, or MWNTs. They have tubes within tubes. They differ from SWNTs in their dimensions and in their corresponding properties.

Despite the safety measures used by those working with nanotubes, Felicity may have been contaminated with nanotubes from her father's work. If this is true, it not now known exactly how the CNTs were passed from her father to her.

Another mystery is whether or not her contamination with these nanotubes is in any way related to her ability, at such a young age, to play what many are calling the best chess games of all time.

Despite all of these setbacks and problems, FAB Felicity is an inspiration to all of us. So, hats off to the Little Lady Of Chess.

Sign up for real-time updates on the Little Lady Of Chess and all current news stories at www.TheTruthNews.edu.

22.

It seemed there was a competition, not to win the game, but to see who could make the fastest responsive move. Although Azure Main's moves were usually computed nearly instantly, a few times Felicity appeared to move more quickly because she could actually move her own pieces on the board. Azure Main's proxy player in the game room, a grandmaster herself, had to take the time to be told the move, to make sure that indeed that was the move, and then to physically move a piece.

Then something startling happened. Felicity moved a queen-side bishop three spaces, and Azure Main paused. The team in the building with the main computer and its servers all stopped what they had been doing. They were stunned as lights flickered and progressed in series on their screens. No new move was instantly forthcoming. Azure Main did not immediately produce a move in reply to the movement of Felicity's bishop. Finally, it indicated a move and the proxy at the board moved a pawn to block the bishop's impact, at least for the moment.

23.

May 6. CCD-London.

Alert! Fab Felcity moves her bishop and stops Azure Main dead in its tracks. At this moment Felicity Bright, the miniature chess phenom, has made a move with her queen-side bishop that has, probably temporarily, brought the master chess computer program, Azure Main, to a standstill. Since its programming was announced as 'unbeatable,' a few years ago, few can remember Azure Main pausing or slowing down during a game. Stay with us for real-time updates as the game progresses.

24.

Five moves later, again Azure Main paused. After two minutes, the single symbol, "=," appeared on the main screen.

The proxy player, quietly, said to herself "Draw?" and then, after having been told that Azure Main had indicated the offer of a draw, said the word, "draw" out loud assuming Felicity heard. Felicity continued to stare at the game board.

"Azure Main is offering you a draw," she said again to Felicity.

Felicity did not move.

Cliff told the officials near to the table, "She is declining the draw."

Back in the control room, several people huddled to discuss Felicity's refusing the draw. Some information was input into the computers and then, in moments, Azure Main provided another move.

25.

May 5. Aleteia Rue (Moscow)

The Little Lady of Chess has just declined a draw offered by the megacomputer chess program Azure Main. The five year old girl, Felicity Agatha Bright, has said, no, we play on. Stay with us for the outcome of this momentous match in chess history. You can click below for all the moves in the game up until the present moment.

26.

Felicity's response time never varied. She moved quickly in reply to each move of the computer program. Thirty-three moves later, the main screen showed one word, "checkmate." The proxy player, staring speechless at the board, laid down Azure Main's king. The program had lost its first game in over two years.

Felicity Agatha Bright would celebrate her sixth birthday in a week. She began to replace all the pieces.

Cliff came over and hugged her. She realized that for now there would not be another game right away.

Cliff stood back and grinned. "You go, girl." he told her. Felicity stared at him, eye to eye. He looked at her and for a moment he thought, *Without speaking, she is saying something, she is saying I am here. My little Full Copy, I so miss your smile.*

The next day Felicity again beat Azure Main. As one news report made clear, she really did not "beat" a computer program. She won a chess game, in effect, against all the people, all the grandmasters, all the experts, everyone, who had a part in making and writing the program.

This win was remarkable for the simple reason that, again, she won. It was even more remarkable because, playing the white pieces, after her first move of a pawn, she moved her queen; and then, after her third move of another pawn, she moved her king. In response to the queen move, Azure Main took several minutes to come up with a response. In response to the king move, after a few moments, the Azure Main screen in the control room said simply "Hibernate." After another minute, Azure Main had produced a responsive move.

27.

The Lynx Network's tagline for the cable news report announced that another game was in progress.

In the Lynx studio, grandmaster Beall Upton was not commenting. He was simply staring at the large screen with the game board and the chess pieces. The host, Maggie Rostal, did not know what question to ask about what was going on, about Upton's silence, so she said, "Is that a typical beginning?"

The camera then showed Upton looking at the screen for a few more moments and then turning to Maggie.

"I have been trying to remember if I have ever seen, ever, such an opening. It is remarkable, if only for its rarity, and, it appears to me, to be utterly senseless. It seems to me this is doom, very soon, for the Little Lady. But I must say, this is intriguing."

28.

Early on, Felicity traded queens, both bishops, some pawns, and both rooks. The board appeared somewhat bare. With both her knights alive and more pawns than Azure Main, she regained her queen. Fifty-seven moves into the game, Felicity had again won. Again the proxy moving Azure Main's pieces agreed with what the pieces on the board made clear, saying to Felicity, "Checkmate, white."

29.

Back in the Lynx news studio, grandmaster Upton was silent again. Maggie's producer pointed to her and then to the grandmaster, signaling her to let the show go on.

"That is somewhat remarkable, isn't it, Mr. Upton?"

"My dear, what you have just seen, as far as I know, has never been done before, never. I am sure you staff and your experts will search all this, but, to me, this is unique. To think that in the beginning, all those moves ago, with the audacious play of the queen and king, the sacrifice of all those pieces, she could see this . . . beyond amazing. As with many of us grandmasters, we can see many options and many moves on many different paths forward. But this? We are all children before this child. This Little Lady is the only chess adult."

The lead headline of the next edition of the New York Tribune Messenger proclaimed "FAB Fantastic," and then provided a detailed history of the development, compiling and writing of the Azure Main program, noting by name the many grandmasters who had contributed to the work.

The Washington Pilot Sun took a different approach, wondering if indeed there are limits to what a computer can do and if Felicity's abilities showed that no computer will ever "think" like a human being. Included was a discussion of the possibility that Goedel's Incompleteness Theorems, proving the limits of every axiomatic system, including mathematics, also established that the limitations of science meant that no computer would ever be able to totally, completely, and accurately mimic human intelligence or human thought.

The UK Daily Servant had a full front page with a picture of Felicity staring at a chess board and the words, "Absolutely FAB-ulous."

The San Antonio Sunbeam proclaimed: "FAB Felicity sends the chess version of Travis's letter from the Alamo - No Draw, Victory or Victory, I Will Never Surrender!" The article included a new version of the famous Texas "Come and Take It" flag with the depiction of a chess queen instead of the cannon.

30.

A few weeks later Cliff and Lucy were watching a television show when Felicity came into the room. She had a piece of paper in her hand.

Cliff and Lucy did not look up. Felicity came and stood by them without making a sound. Cliff looked over and saw the piece of paper. Felicity reached out to hand it to him. Lucy was now watching, unbelieving.

"Darling," was all Cliff said to Felicity as he handed the piece of paper to Lucy. It was the diagram of doctor Zarkov's new system for removing material from a human body, human blood, and a human brain. Felicity had added a checkmark to the drawing.

Felicity sat down in a chair across from Cliff and Lucy and looked at them both, calmly and without turning away. She did not speak or make any sound, and continued to stare at them.

"Same question," Cliff told Lucy. "What do we do now?"

Lucy bit her lip. "It's not just Felicity. What if it could help those children. Look at all our letters. There are hundreds, from moms and dads all over, and grandmothers and grandfathers whose child or grandchild has been hurt by vaccines.

31.

June 30. From Universal Point website magazine:

You Are Rolling Vaccine Dice With Your Child's Health & Life

by Gary McClure, J.D., Ph.D.

No matter what the odds, the stats or the probabilities, you are gambling when you get vaccinated, and when you have your child vaccinated, You are rolling the dice and playing vaccine roulette withr your child's health, and very life.

To say we all must do this for the "common good" is imposing a morality on all of us. Enforcing this view on an entire population with legislation and regulations is using the power of the state to force a view of a particular morality on everyone. The Pro Vaxx mantra is "Yes, 1 in 1000 or 1 in 100,000 or 1 in a million will die and Yes, that could be you or your child or baby, but this is required for all of us, so there will be this legally-mandated sacrifice. It's worth it - at least to those of us who don't die."

The government, which bottom line is one group of people in power telling others not in power what to do, accepts the my-body-my-self-my-choice ideology when it serves their purposes for gaining support from certain segments of the population.

But when that thinking conflicts with a drive to impose vaccinations on everyone, to inject substances into human bodies, they make a blahblahbalh excuse and talk about "common good."

For controlling population numbers and weeding out those with certain conditions, my-body-my-self-my-choice is their dogma, their law, a law that allows for government control of the end of life for some very young and some very old. Ironically, they champion a mother's killing of her child, even after it is born; but once the child has made it out of the clinic, or business, or hospital, then that same mother is forced to vaccinate that child – or lose it to the state.

Comments of the article:

FUNFOLK34: one hour ago:

Spot on! That group of smart folks called "the State" tells us we can force materials, and mercury, and adjuvants, and all the contaminants found in vaccines into that child, and push the needle in with the power of the State.

SciGal123: one day ago:

Science? Really CpD20? Just search this online: 'Symposium on the reproducibility and reliability of biomedical research'. You'll find that a noted editor of a noted journal says tons of what is called "scientific" and in published papers is simply wrong; and maybe even as much as half is just not true. It it's wrong, and it's not true, why is this alleged 'research' being done? You must hate it, but deep down you know, FollowMoneyHoney speaks the truth.

CpD20 • two days ago:

Of course there are risks associated with vaccines, and no one is saying otherwise. There is no human activity that is totally safe. Practially every job, every thing we do, work, play, daily routine, has risks. But settled science shows us-without doubt- that all the risks of all vaccines are very, very small. So small that you really cannot conclusively determine if anything that has been reported is actually a result of the administration of a vaccine.

Lollipop: one day ago:

Check out the numerous medical doctors who refuse to have their own children vaccinated. I personally know a recent graduate who has just completed residency in a large city. He and his wife have two little children. They study everything - and they are waiting-their little ones have received no vaccines. And I have found information, though I don't know them personally, of some medical doctors, people with MD degrees, around the country who are now going public and who have not vaccinated their kids.

CpD20: one day ago:

The drug and vaccine corporations do not make that much money from vaccines; and much of that money is then used for further research on vaccines, both existing ones and new ones that will help prevent even more diseases. Safety is as much a concern to these companies as is profits. If they did not care about us, all of us, they would focus on many other drugs and other research that would be infinitely more profitable.

FollowMoneyHoney: two days ago

Sorry, but it seems all those telling us to "do it for the team" for what they spout is the "common good," out of what they say is simply "common sense," they are all making money. Not just some dollars, but billion$s of dollars. Not just here, but all over the world. And follow some of that money to officeholders and politicians, and rulers in many countries, who, amazingly, sound like the companies puppets; and follow it to researchers who- hard to believe ! – come up with 'proven' results that support the BigVaxx and BigPharma companies who are preaching the common good, while their profits go up and their shareholders all make money.

Yugyug3: two days ago:

If it weren't for the billion$s involved and the payments to physicians, perhaps "trusting" those who supposedly have our interests at heart, who seek the truth, and who know the truth, *would make sense. But thank God for this internet-the truth will out.*

TruthDude33: three days ago

Come on, CpD, sure, there may have been a time when caring doctors wanted to comfort and heal their patients and honest scientists only sought truth, but that is centuries ago. Some hundreds of years back these 'caregivers' and 'truth seekers' became servants of power. Bad enough. But more recently they, and folks like you, have become 'soldiers' of power, Internet search C.S. Lewis and "power over nature;" and Max Horkheimer and "obedience to power."

CpD20: five days ago:

There is no peer-reviewed scientific study that proves that these stories, however many there may be out there, are factual or anything other than mere 'anecdotal' tales. There is no good scientific evidence of a link between metals or preservatives from vaccines and autism spectrum disorders. And there is no evidence, scientific evidence, that chelation can successfully treat autism.

BNDFKCShn: a week ago:

One of our children, unfortunately, accidentally ingested some old paint materials and was diagnosed with lead poisoning. Luckily there is a treatment available – from decades ago, called chelation, and now our child is fine. It is not an easy treatment and must be done under strict medical supervision at a licensed facility by medical doctors and nurses. I met several mothers while we were at that facility. They were not there because of any accidental metal poisoning, and they all had the same story about their children: healthy child, most toddlers, doctor visit for check up and scheduled vaccine updates, within hours or a few days brain dysfunction, autism, whatever you might want to call it.

32.

Felicity was lying flat on a full-body cushioned support staring at the ceiling, in a room filled with machines, equipment, lights, screens, controls, lines, and cables everywhere, full of nurses and doctors and technicians.

The exit and return lines for the autologous blood system had been placed within her blood vessels and everything was ready to begin. Tiny suction lines for interstitial fluid had been placed in her right thigh and abdomen. It would take twenty-seven minutes for blood to be pumped from Felicity's veins, treated to remove the metals and carbon nanotubes, and then returned back to her system. It would take slightly more time for the fluid from the interstitium to be treated and returned. Most of the people in the room were either engrossed watching a screen or scurrying around from one machine to another.

"Before we have to leave this room," said Lucy, "We are going to pray."

Everyone in the room paused as Lucy stood on one side of Felicity and Cliff stood on the other. They each held one of her hands. Quietly, Lucy sang.

Guardian angel, go with me.

Hold me close and comfort me.
Stay with me and be my guide,
Never ever leave my side.
Angel dear I love you.
I know you love me too.
Bring me safe home to love God with you.

Then Cliff leaned over and blessed her:

"May God bless you and keep you, precious child, and always hold you safe in the palm of His hand until we see you again."

After Lucy had also blessed Felicity, they stood back, both with tears in their eyes. Then they walked out and went into an observation room with live-feed real-time output from cameras in the treatment room.

Doctor Zarkov turned from Felicity and spoke to Cliff and Lucy via the camera system.

"We can stop the autologous blood system and the interstitial system at any time," doctor Zarkov said. "Today, we will do about a half hour and then analyze the results. Felicity should feel no pain, but we will monitor her continuously."

Two doctors and two nurses, along with the several technicians, hovered around Felicity. Technicians stood at the various machines and devices while others watched the screens.

Thirty-eight minutes later doctor Zarkov said, "Done," as he turned off the main pumps of the blood system and the pump for the interstitial fluid evacuation and return. Others continued to watch the screens and monitors that continued to indicate Felicity's bodily functions. Blood pressure, inspiration rate, pulse, everything was normal.

After the lines had all been removed, the various tubes disconnected, and the machines turned off, Felicity sat up. Doctor Zarkov turned around and smiled at Lucy and Cliff, pleased that, evidently, Felicity had felt no pain.

"She is one tough little girl. Tomorrow," he said. "Tomorrow we will have all this analyzed and see if it worked."

33.

The next day they all returned to the research facility. A team of doctors and psychologists were going to test, and track if possible, any change in Felicity's cognitive abilities and some motor functions, both sensorimotor and psychomotor functioning. The hope was that by doing both types of tests, if there was a brain basis for some of the cognitive impairments, a correlation could be developed.

Felicity, Lucy and Cliff sat in chairs at a conference table.

"Well, seems like she is fine," said Cliff.

"Maybe it's hope, maybe a mother's dream," said Lucy. "But it seems to me she is more here. I can't describe it. But I feel this. I think she is communicating with us. Not trying, but doing. Just in a touch, in a look."

Almost imperceptibly, slowly, and then clearly moving, Felicity turned toward Lucy and looked at her.

"You go girl !" said Cliff and then he hugged Felicity.

The four doctors entered the room. Doctor Yarl smiled seeing Cliff hug Felicity.

"We have some results from yesterday," announced doctor Zarkov. "I hate to get your hopes up, but this may be good news." He clicked a projector and a graph appeared on the board. "We actually did remove aluminum, iron, and carbon. Both from the blood and from the interstitial fluid. Both. And from her brain. And there is another surprise. We also removed ethylmercury."

"What is 'ethylmercury' ?" asked Cliff.

"Ethylmercury is an organic derivative of mercury. Some vaccines, probably some that Lucy has received over her lifetime, used a preservative called 'Thimerosal' and ethylmercury is a product of the digestion, metabolizing in the human gut, of this preservative. We don't think this mercury came from any other source, because vaccines for children and Felicity's vaccines no longer have this mercury-containing preservative, except for some flu vaccines. And she has no tooth fillings with mercury in them."

"I do have those fillings," said Lucy. "And I hate to say it, in most of my teeth. Way too much chewing gum and candy as a kid. And Cliff and I get our flu vaccines every year, like a yearly religious ritual. Even though he hates needles. So the process worked?"

"We know we took some things out of her blood and out of the fluid. The amounts are infinitesimal, measured in parts of micrograms. But we did get them out. And most important, we see no adverse effect for Felicity. We are pretty sure she did not feel any unusual pain. She is one tough little girl."

"So now we go again?" Cliff was curious.

Doctor Chan spoke now. He was very serious. "Cliff and Lucy. It may not be that simple. Yes, we put together this whole system and yes we did successfully remove some substances from Felicity's blood and from the fluid. Then that same blood and that cleaned up fluid was successfully reintroduced into her body. Perhaps with some other patient, in some other scenario, we might all be patting ourselves on the back and telling doctor Alexis this is remarkable. But that is not the whole story and all of us believe we must tell you this."

The other three doctors nodded their agreement.

Doctor Zarkov spoke. "All of us on this team still know almost nothing about what is going on, what is happening with Felicity, and if any of this is doing any good. We all agree we must tell you that we cannot recommend you proceed."

"I think we understand all you have said and all we have read and all you have done," said Lucy. "But I want you to know, you all are only part of the team. God is the captain of Felicity's team. We have prayed and we will pray now."

When Lucy finished speaking, Felicity got up from her chair. Everyone stared at her. She walked to the end of the room and stared at the screen. Then she bowed her head.

34.

Cliff, Lucy, and Felicity were walking down the corridor to the treatment room. Felicity stopped in front of a glass window and stared at her own reflection. Cliff and Lucy paused in the corridor and waited.

"Fifth time, fifth time, darlin'," Cliff said to Felicity.

The third and fourth treatment cycles had removed greater amounts of the metals, the ehtylmercury, and CNTs than the first run. There had been no side effects, no pain, nothing. For the second, third and fourth treatments, Felicity had shown no response other than, on her own, to go and sit on the cushioned platform, without being asked, and position herself for all the various preparations. Significantly larger amounts of the metals, the CNTs, and the ethylmercury were removed.

Everyone involved was startled when Felicity's post-treatment cognitive tests results did not change for treatments two and three, and some indicators improved.

Standing in the corridor, Lucy spoke to Felicity as she continued to stare at her reflection. "They are going to go over an hour. But you know you can have them stop at any time."

In the treatment room, again Cliff and Lucy prayed, holding Felicity's hands. As they had before, everyone present stopped what they were doing and stood quietly as they listened to the prayer.

God her Father, Father in heaven,
Father be with her evermore.
Jesus her brother, Jesus beside her,
Jesus be with her evermore.
Holy Spirit, Spirit Holy,
Spirit be with her evermore.

An hour and fifteen minutes later Lucy reentered the treatment room and went and held Felicity's limp hand as they removed all the tubes and lines. Felicity moved and then gripped Lucy's hand.

Am I imagining this? Lucy thought.

Then Felicity gripped Lucy's hand tighter. Lucy looked at her and Felicity was looking back, eye to eye. She had not done this for all the years since the 'vaccine adverse event'.

"Cliff, come here, now!" Lucy spoke so loudly that everyone turned to her. Cliff hurried in.

Felicity turned her head to look at Cliff and then turned back to Lucy and said, "Mommy."

With tears welling up, through her laughter, Lucy said. "Yes, Mommy! Yes, I am your Mommy! Yes."

No one in the room moved. Everyone was absolutely silent, staring at Felicity.

Cliff was now holding Felicity's other hand and she turned to him and said, "Don't you fussing, Daddy! I'm Felicity."

Cliff hugged her. "Yes, you are Felicity, our Felicity."

Smiling again, Felicity said to Lucy, "You go girl!"

Cliff realized Felicity had known when he said that to her before and after all those chess games.

Everyone crowded around Felicity's bed. Doctors and nurses and technicians were crying, smiling, and laughing at the same time.

"I wanted to say 'I love you.' I love you both." Felicity was calm, serene. She sat there holding her parents hands.

Doctor Zarkov approached the bed.

"You are doctor Alexis Hans Zarkov," Felicity said.

All doctor Zarkov could do was smile. "My little lady," he said, "the pleasure is all mine, all mine."

35.

On the ride home, Lucy sat in the back seat next to Felicity while Cliff drove. Felicity held both of Lucy's hands in hers.

"Mommy, I was there. All the time. It was me. I heard everything you and Daddy said, with all those doctors and all those other people and nurses. I read all those words. I just could not talk. I don't know why. But now I can."

Lucy could tell Felicity was still not perfectly lucid, but it was as if she had just come out of this huge fog cloud and things were getting more and more clear.

"It's working," Lucy told Cliff. "Whatever they are doing, whatever is happening, it is working."

"Darlin', daddy loves you," was all Cliff said.

"Love you too, daddy," Felicity responded.

"You just keep saying that, just keep saying that, all the way home."

36.

After two more long treatment cycles, with even more metals and CNTs removed, the results of Felicity's cognitive and intelligence tests were amazing. She truly was being changed by the treatment. No one wanted to use the word "healed," but there was no better word. "Detoxed," "cleaned," "improved," "flushed out," "rejuvenated," all came to mind, but "healed" became the word of choice.

When they arrived at the treatment facility one morning three weeks later, they were directed to a large meeting room and there were four times as many people there as usual.

Doctor Zarkov walked over and took Felicity's hand. "Do you remember me?" he asked her.

Felicity looked at him and smiled. "Yes, you're doctor Zarkov. You talk a lot."

Everyone laughed.

"My little lady, believe me, you talk ever so much better than I do. And now many more people everywhere will hear you. Do you know why all these people are here?"

"To fix me?" she asked.

"No, no. Some of them already believed in miracles, but some of them had to see for themselves. You are a miracle."

Felicity was embarrassed. "No, God did my miracle. Are you going to start talking again now? With the screen?"

All eyes were on Felicity as doctor Zarkov replied.

"If that is OK with you, yes. Can we all sit down over here?"

Clfif and Lucy sat down on chairs at a table at the front of the room, with Felicity between them.

"Everyone, this is Felicity Agatha Bright and her parents, Lucy and Cliff. You may know her as the 'Little Lady of Chess,' or FAB-ulous Felicity. I assure you she is all of that and more."

37.

By the end of that week the news about Felicity had spread throughout the facility and beyond. More cycles, more material removal, more improved cognitive functions and increased communications with Felicity. Again, the Little Lady of Chess was worldwide news.

"Daddy," I knew what was going on, all the time.

"All of it?" Cliff asked her, unbelieving.

"Yes. Well, not when I was little."

Cliff laughed out loud. "When you were little? Before you grew up to be six? Now really grown up almost seven?"

"Daddy!" Felicity understood the humor. "Things were just there. Clear. Like when I watched you and uncle John play chess and I saw what you did and I knew. The men could only move the way they were supposed to. All over the board. And when I heard you and mommy read and then I read it and I could read. It was so quick."

Lucy made a comment. "But now you don't play chess like you did anymore."

"I know," Felicity told Lucy. "I can't do it. I remember the games and being there and moving the men and looking at the boards and all of it. But it is like all the ways to do it are not there in front of me anymore. I can't see that far in my mind now."

"And all those tests and meeting with doctors and all that?"

"I was there. I saw it all and heard it all. I think I got to know what they were saying. I could remember it all. Like with all those chess games. And now I don't know it."

"Here's what we know. You are our Felicity," Cliff said. "And we are happy with you just the way you are."

"Me too," said Felicity as she hugged Lucy.

38.

August 15: The T News

There is incredible news today about Felicity Agatha Bright, the little girl who has played chess at a grandmaster level for two years now. Some say she is the greatest chess player of all time, particularly after she beat the Azure Main computer chess program that was believed to be unbeatable. Once it had been perfected, no one even came close to beating the Azure Main. Not until "FAB Felicity" came on the chess scene.

Many in the scientific and medical communities believed her amazing mental abilities were somehow related to her being poisoned with carbon nanotubes with which her father had been contaminated in his work. After her exposure, Felicity's brain function and nervous system were diminished and impacted in many ways. But there was also an astonishing effect on several functions that some believed made it possible for her to play chess. Carbon nanotubes – called "CNTs" - are tiny little carbon structures that are so small they can go anywhere in the human body, even into the brain and individual cells.

Now, in a revolutionary new process, it has been announced by Doctor Alexis Zarkov that the bulk of the CNTs have been successfully removed from Felicity and she is beginning again to exhibit normal brain functioning. A side effect of the Zarkov

Process is, apparently, that Felicity has lost the ability to play chess at the grandmaster level.

FIDE is investigating whether or not Felicity's accomplishments are to be recognized officially, due to the presence of what are now being termed "unnatural" enhancers," the carbon nanotubes.

The chess comet, FAB Felicity, may have passed and flamed out, but, thanks to science and the new process for dealing with nanotube removal, she can again lead a normal life.

39.

"I'll bet you are getting bored with these meetings and all the removal procedures," doctor Zarkov told Felicity.

"No way, doctor Zark," Felicity replied. Then she tried to be serious, "Isn't 'Zark' a good name?" she asked him.

Before he could reply, everyone in the room laughed. He knew right then that this name was going to stick.

"I am honored, my little lady," he said as he bowed to her. "And do I have news for you and your parents."

Cliff looked at Lucy as if to say, *What's this all about*?

Lucy stared back with her hands raised silently saying, *I don't have a clue.*

"Lucy do you remember early on you told us about all the, what you called 'natural treatments' things and 'God's medicine' you had learned about and you were beginning to do, all the things for Down Syndrome children?"

"Yes, and we have done them all these months, all these years now."

"Well, let me show you some photos and then let me show you some test results. You know there are few little girls on this earth who have had their bodies scanned, and tested, and probed, and stuck, and studied as much as Felicity. And now we have more than books about her. Volumes and volumes. Now just look at these."

Doctor Zarkov began showing a series of photos on the large screen in the room. It included photos from every time she had been at the research facility and some from news stories about her over the last three years.

"That's me!" Felicity said gleefully.

Lucy saw it immediately. Cliff turned to her. "What am I looking at?"

Lucy asked doctor Zarkov, "Could you show the first two and the last two photos in sequence?"

After a few moments, doctor Zarakov said, "Here you go," and the images of Felicity as a three year old appeared on the screen followed a few moments later with two recent photos.

"Oh, wow!" said Cliff.

"Wow is right," said Lucy. "She's not just growing, she's changing."

"What?" said Felicity. "Me, changing" How?"

It was clear that her eyes, her ears, and her hands were definitely changed, along with other features.

"When this became more and more evident, and many of us who are working with her noticed it, we thought there is more here than simply the changes associated with normal growth. And we realized we had not done the gene testing for some months and so we ran them again. What you are about to see is truly amazing."

The screen showed the results for Felicity's chromosomes.

"What is this?" asked Lucy.

"Here is an old test, the first one we did," said doctor Zarkov. "Your little lady, as you knew, was 'full copy' Trisomy 21." He switched to the recent test results. "And now, she is not."

"Now what?" asked Felicity. "Am I fixed?"

"You are precious," said doctor Zarkov.

40.

"He's here!" Felicity announced as the doorbell rang. She got there before Cliff or Lucy. She opened the door and there stood Radoslav Kolenda.

Bowing to her, he said, "Little Lady, it is my pleasure to see you again."

"Uncle Rad!" Felicity almost yelled it. Then she hugged him and they came into the living room.

Cliff and Lucy walked in and he embraced Lucy.

"Funny how this all started those years ago," Lucy said. "How is your mother?"

"Still maxing all those cognitive ability tests. Docs cannot believe what she is doing at 94 years old. Really, ninety-nine plus percentile. But that's not the best. She's still lucky."

"Lucky?" Cliff asked.

"Bingo, yes bingo. She wins all the time. Gives the prizes away mostly, unless they include chocolate. Then she shares."

"Speaking of chocolate," Radodslav reached in a pocket and brought out a Cadbury's bar. "Straight from London," he said as he handed it to Felicity.

"Oh, thank you," she said. Then she looked at Lucy. "Later? After lunch?"

"Yes. Later. A little bit only." Lucy was so pleased Felicity had asked.

Radoslav noticed a game board with checkers on the coffee table in front of the sofa he was sitting on.

He asked Felicity, "Do you play checkers?"

"Well, I am learning, not so good yet. Daddy beats me most of the time. It's not like when I could do chess."

After many cycles of the cleansing of her body, with the detoxing and the removal of metals and other materials, Felicity had not been able to play chess anymore as she had in the past.

During a past visit, Lucy had told Radoslav, "It is like she cannot see all that she used to see, like the mental pathways have been shortened, or turned off."

"And now she smiles again and laughs," said Radoslav. He remembered back to his first meeting with the tiny chess prodigy who did not look him in the eye. "I think I will be happy with this Felicity. To me, she is just as 'fabulous'. "

Radoslav turned to Felicity. "Can I ask you a question?"

"Sure," said Felicity as she arranged the checkers to begin a game.

"Do you remember? What it was like to play chess? All those games?"

"I remember a lot, except I can't play like that anymore. I knew what was going on. Like I heard everyone talking. And I didn't talk or the words didn't come out. And after watching uncle John and Daddy play, it was just there. I could see. I could see like all the moves the men could make, all these things that could happen, like close and way far away, and it was just there, all of it. Clear. Very clear. And I could see where I was going and where the other players were going, like all the paths through a forest that were possible, and what was at the end. It was like lit up and, well, easy. Like looking down all the streets of a big city at once."

"But no more?" asked Radoslav.

"Yes. It's like it turned off. Like my head isn't so busy anymore."

Lucy spoke. "She still has all she had before. She reads and plays and bounces around, but it's like all that intense thinking doesn't happen now. And she kisses us again."

"And you have given me and everyone so many of those smiles," Radoslav told Felicity. "Do you have any left?"

She looked at him very serious and he thought he may have offended her. Then she broke out laughing.

"And here's one more for you!" she said, smiling at him. "Now, checkers?"

Epilogue

"And this year's Nobel Prize for Medicine is awarded to Doctor Alexis Hans Zarkov. The breakthrough poisoning detoxing methods that he developed and which have been so successful have been extended in what seems a miracle to provide an amazingly effective cancer treatment. His theory about cancer metastases, questioned at first, has proven to be another miracle.

In an interview, when one journalist mentioned T.S. Kuhn's seminal work, *The Structure Of Scientific Revolutions* and referred to the new body paradigm for anatomy and medicine as the 'Zarkov paradigm,' he corrected her and told her that posterity will know it as the 'Felicity Paradigm.' This is a reference to the little girl who was known as the 'Little Lady of Chess,' Felicity Agatha Bright, and the research done on her that led to doctor Zarkov's breakthroughs.

September 15. CCD News

Reports out of Japan today say that a child prodigy being called the 'Little Man Of Go' has been found in Osaka. Four year old Suro Yatushisa, who has been autistic since age three, has beaten the tenth ranking Go master in the world in a game that took five hours. Little Suro is autistic and many have immediately compared him to the Little Lady of Chess, Felicity Bright.